Isabel Anderson

Illustrated by Loma Tilders

Revised USA Edition © 2003 Published by Scholastic Inc.
By arrangement with Reed International Books, Australia Pty Ltd.

Dad and Me and the Road Ahead
0-439-64908-0

Printed in China by QP International Ltd

10 9 8 7 6 5 4 3 2 1 04 05 06

Contents

Chapter One

Thanh and Dad

In the car, Dad keeps a bottle of water wrapped in a towel. He continually worries about running out of gas. It's a long, straight road and not many cars pass by. I sleep in the back seat. I sleep with the seat belt loose (but secure, I think) across my body. I think I won't be able to sleep, and for a long time I can't. It's a smooth ride but there is something that hums under the seat, which gives me a whirring head. When I wake I'm sure I haven't slept, because of the thudding pain behind my eyes.

Dad is sympathetic about my headache. He suggests that we stop to eat. He is tired of driving but would rather drive hard all day and have a good sleep at night. We have a long way to go, he insists. But we do stop to eat. I have a big orange juice and two lots of toasted sandwiches. Dad has the same plus coffee. We both feel revived after our stop. I sit in the front seat. I suck barley sugars and flick around on the radio until I find songs we both like.

Ooh, ooh, I can't get it out of my head.

I howl the 'ooh, oohs' out of the window and Dad smiles at me because I'm having a good time, not complaining. I unwrap the bottle from its thin towel and take a few big gulps. We are both feeling very relaxed. Dad looks concerned from time to time about the level of gas. He keeps checking whether I want to hop in the back and have a sleep. I tell him not to worry, I'm a big boy. I'll speak up when I need a rest. But I do doze off and when I open a sleepy eye, I see Dad pulling up to a halt. I sit up quickly.

"What is it? Are we there?" I ask, although I hardly know where 'there' is and we couldn't possibly be there yet. I peer through the windscreen, squinting at the setting sun.

"It's the ferry. We're lucky. We've arrived just in time. The ferry is in," Dad says as he winds down the window and pops his head out. "Hope we're not going to miss out though," he mumbles.

"Miss out?" I query.

"Well, there are a lot more cars than I thought there'd be," Dad confides.

I feel a little panicky but try to appear calm. Dad is such a pessimist. The line of cars starts to move. I stretch my head out of the window to check our progress. The ferryman is waving confidently and there are only three cars in front of us.

In the distance, I can see the deep sea that we are to cross. The sun on the sea makes it blue and sparkling. Almost good enough to swim in, except that it would be far too cold.

"We'll be fine. We'll get on," I assure Dad, "and it doesn't matter if we don't, does it?"

Dad explains that it's very important that we get on the ferry because otherwise we'll have to backtrack to the nearest town and wait. Dad is not the patient type and he does have a deadline, so when he finally brakes and comes to a stop on board the ferry, I am relieved. Dad nearly smiles except that his face is caught up in a frown.

I immediately hop out of the car. I don't want to hang around with cars and cargo and no view. I want to go up on deck and watch the ferry pull out of the harbor, leaving land behind. I like to watch where I've been. On trains and buses, I always sit with my back toward the driver. Dad stays in the car. He says he is going to check the map. As I slam the car door, I notice he is fumbling with the cell phone. I don't think he's used one before. I can't tell him that he'd be lucky to reach anyone out here. He tells me not to stray too far. I grin a little at this but not so Dad would notice.

I like being alone on deck. I watch the people on the quayside effortlessly do their jobs as if they've done them a thousand times before. I watch the cars that missed the ferry turn around and head back on the road through the forest. I watch the sun get lower until it no longer streams through the pine trees in the forest. It is getting cool so I hug my jacket to my chest. There are other people on deck now, but they are in a group together, so I am really alone.

When the harbor has faded from view, I go inside. I join the line for food and buy Dad some coffee. I buy us each a chocolate bar, too. Dad loves chocolate. Then I tramp down the narrow stairs back to the car below. But there is no one there. The car is locked. Dad must be up on the next level. I stop to fix the lid on the coffee cup. It'll be cold if I don't find him soon, I think. I look in every direction but it's hard to search when you're balancing a coffee cup. I go up to the next level, thinking Dad might be lining up for food (chips would go down well), but he isn't there. I check everywhere without drawing attention to myself. He must be out on the deck, taking in the fresh air.

I swing the doors open and walk around the deck, clasping the coffee cup and my jacket, which is still billowing in the cold wind. It is nearly dark now and I am getting annoyed with Dad. When I finally find him huddled in a corner with the cell phone, I don't apologize for the lukewarm coffee (as I'd been planning to). Dad doesn't want to hear anything from me. In fact, he raises his hand as if to stop me from opening my mouth and interrupting a conversation he's not even having. He is pressing the buttons on the phone then shaking it. I leave the coffee on the deck and wander over to the rail. I don't look behind me but I know Dad has not noticed the coffee at his feet. I rip open the chocolate bars and eat both of them. I am still starving. I stare at the dark sea beneath me. I can't wait to get back in the car where it is comfortable and I have Dad next to me.

When we get close to the south island, we sit and wait in the car below, eating. As we drive off the ferry, I wind the car window down all the way. The car is thick with the smell of chips. Like on the ferry, the cool breeze makes the tips of my ears cold and my eyes water.

As we hit the road, Dad accelerates and we are free of the other ferry cars. We are looking for a hotel in the nearest town, which is only a few miles away. We each look at a side of the road and first to spot a cheap hotel is the winner.

"There!" I yell, excitedly, pointing to a flat clump of units and a brightly lit neon sign. "Home for the night, Dad." I win again.

Chapter Two

Dad and Thanh

We leave the hotel early in the morning. Thanh checks under the beds before we leave, in case we've left anything behind. I like to start driving before the sun is up. I pay for the room we slept in the night before and we stop for breakfast after the sun has risen. Thanh starts to nod off to sleep again. I feel guilty making him get up so early, but we can get such a long way before any traffic joins us on the road that I feel it is worth it. Thanh says it's worth it too. He doesn't mind getting up early. It doesn't matter to him.

Now Thanh is complaining because he needs his breakfast. Perhaps that is making him tired, too. I pull over to the side of the road. I've spotted a cafe where the truck drivers stop. We can eat here. I stop abruptly and this wakens Thanh with a jolt. He complains about being cold until we are comfortably seated in a cosy booth in the diner and have plates of hot breakfast in front of us. I don't know how I've never noticed how much Thanh can eat.

"I like it here," says Thanh about the diner. He talks more than I can remember, too. "I reckon I'd be quite good being a truck driver on the road. Sitting up high in the cab. Looking at the little cars below ... and you have all those wheels, those huge tires ..." Thanh pauses to tear at his toast, then he keeps on talking, until I interrupt to agree with him.

"You know, I think it would be great to just drive all day, with no boss, no office – just being a truck driver. Stopping when you wanted," I suggest. "Stopping at diners for breakfast. Pulling over to the side of the road for a snooze, that sort of thing. Eating candy for energy ..."

There was no stopping our conversation. We went on like this for quite a while. Rambling on, watching the other diners, making comments about their appearance and habits and generally enjoying each other's company. I completely forgot what we were doing here.

I do a few exercises for my back before I get back in the car. Thanh seems to find the sight of me funny but he launches into some frantic exercise of his own – running on the spot, arms flailing powerfully. Just being silly.

It's not good to sit in a car all day. My arms ache at the elbows from holding the steering wheel for long periods at high speed. Our thighs ache, too – from being horizontal. And we both got headaches from gas fumes, I'm sure.

"Not long now," I assure Thanh.

Thanh straightens his shirt and adjusts his cap. Exertion gives Thanh a dishevelled appearance. He smiles impishly, "I know. Not long now."

'Not long now' is just a line we repeat to each other. It is a line like 'We're nearly there' or 'Just around the next corner' or 'One more hill to go', you know the kind of thing. Thanh likes those kinds of games and I think I'm getting better at them. Only this time, I really mean it. We aren't far from the very south of the island and that is our destination. We'll be there by mid-afternoon, if everything goes to schedule.

Chapter Three

Thanh Wakes Up

I am sleeping when it happens. Although because of that humming noise in my head, I feel that I am not really sleeping at all. I hear the screech of the tires and I immediately lurch upright, hanging onto the seat belt. Dad is shouting, although at first I can't make out what he is saying. Then he slumps back in his seat and speaks to me.

"It's all right," he tells me, "it's all right. Are you OK?" He swings round to look at me.

"Yeah sure, I'm OK. What happened?"

There is steam coming out of the engine, I can see that much. And we are on the side of the road, next to a flat field.

"I knew this car wouldn't last," says Dad. "Let's have a look." I must have looked doubtful because Dad added, "Just because we can." We have no idea about cars. We know we are doomed but we'll look anyway.

We climb out of the car and look under the bonnet at the engine. We stand back as the steam subsides. We have no idea what is wrong with the car. We wait a while, then Dad tries to start the car. As we thought, it won't start. In fact it hardly makes a noise.

"It doesn't matter," I tell Dad. "Why don't we get to the next town and find a garage? Someone could tow us."

"I'll try this," says Dad. He is punching numbers into the cell phone but of course it isn't working. "You know, this thing has never worked properly. I don't know why they gave it to an idiot like me." Dad sighs, giving me a silly look, "Just what we need, huh?"

We decide to walk to the next town, which Dad thinks is where we are going anyway. He checks the map one more time and he is right. The next town is the small mining town of Landfill. Dad goes on about how we could wait for hours for another car to come by, and what if they don't want to help us? Dad is a pessimist.

We put some of our stuff from the suitcases into our smaller backpacks. We heave the packs onto our shoulders and set off along the edge of the road.

I find a long stick on the ground. This is my walking stick. "I'll find one for you too, Dad," I tell him, and I keep an eye out for a stick. I spot one in the distance and race toward it. Dad is anxiously peering along the road, looking for signs of life – a house, a car, someone riding a horse even.

"Here Dad." I hold out the stick. Dad tries out the stick but it is too short and he says he'd rather put his thumbs on his shoulder straps. That is comfortable for him, he says.

All this walking is good exercise, better than sitting in a car, but it is starting to get dark. Dad eyes the sky and frowns. "We'd be there by now, if only that car had done its job," says Dad grimly.

But I am cheerful. I like being in the middle of nowhere with just my dad. I am not worried at all.

"It doesn't matter, Dad, honestly," I say.

"Of course it matters, Thanh. Why do you keep saying it doesn't?" Dad snaps at me.

I don't respond and Dad doesn't expect me to. I don't want to think about how I feel (which is not great), so I concentrate on walking faster, building a good rhythm between my walking stick and the deliberately large paces I am taking.

Eventually a car does give us a lift and soon I spot a small town – a small, ugly town but I spot it first. Dad and I feel quite cheery now, sitting in the back seat of a local's car, but I don't feel like speaking. I don't like to say things in front of strangers even if they are friendly. I don't want to say anything rude about this town either, and that's all you could say by the look of it. Still, they seem friendly. The driver tells us his name, Bob, and doesn't even ask for ours. He tells us about the town, how it's changed far too much. I look out of the window and Dad mutters responses.

Chapter Four

Gordon's Garage

I am relieved to reach the town despite the look of it. It's barren around here and deserted. Thanh hasn't said anything, which is probably not a good sign. Landfill is a mining town and the surrounding countryside looks like it's been mined for plant and animal life too. I wasn't expecting a town quite as unappealing as this one or I would have had second thoughts about bringing Thanh along. I suppose it's an experience for him.

No doubt it doesn't matter to him.

We stop at the hotel where we sign in. It's in the main street of small timber houses and scrubby trees. We head toward the nearest garage. This is where we've been told we'll find Gordon, who has a towtruck. I wonder, in a place this deserted and sleepy, if Gordon hasn't already finished for the day. But we are in luck. Big Gordon is not too pleased to see us at first. He is just heading home for the day and we turn up. Despite this he is happy enough to help us.

Gordon is a tall, sandy-haired man with large gritty hands. He disappears to put on some dark green work overalls before hopping into the truck. Gordon leans across the bench seat and pushes open the door. Thanh scrambles in then turns to me, smiling broadly. The truck is disappointingly small and it smells like a wet dog.

Gordon, who must be sensitive to the state of his cab, quickly explains, "Bit of a damp roof. Can't do anything about it."

Gordon turns on the ignition, the truck clunks into action and we head back along the road to pick up our car. Gordon breaks the silence in the truck by offering us some mints. "They help me see in the dark."

He is curious about us.

"Have you come to get a job in the mine?" he asks.

"No, no," I reply. "I've come to do a safety check at the mine."

"Oh, you're from the government then?" he mutters.

I don't want to say yes because of the tone in his voice, but I do. I can't help it if I am not going to be popular. I believe in the importance of my job. I shouldn't need to feel ashamed of anything.

"Good on you," Gordon responds, surprisingly. "Someone's got to check the place is safe."

Because I am so pleased with this response, I ignore Gordon and he turns his attention to Thanh.

"Summer vacation?" he asks.

Thanh nods and grins. I can tell he likes Gordon – he can't stop grinning. He might even be a bit proud of me.

I can see our abandoned car and am just about to call out when Thanh beats me to it. "There it is. Over there!" Thanh calls out excitedly. "It's still there, Dad." In the glare of the truck lights sits our forlorn-looking car, waiting for us by the flat field.

Chapter Five

Things That Matter I

The following morning, Dad starts work and I trundle along, too. I have no idea of what to expect from the day. Can't imagine what'll happen. I'll probably end up minding Dad's stuff in a tiny office while Dad does the exciting stuff, even though he says it's not exciting at all.

On the way to the mine office, we stop at Gordon's garage to check the car. Dad wants to know whether we can leave the following day. I can tell that he doesn't think we will.

"Forget it," says Gordon, confirming his doubts. "I'll need to get parts in from Marley. That'll take about two days. You won't be leaving here in a hurry. How long were you planning to stay anyway?"

"Just a day or so," Dad says. He shrugs his shoulders and looks at me, meaningfully. But he speaks to Gordon. "We were going to head back tomorrow, go to the coast on the way – have a bit of a vacation. Thanh loves the beach."

We tell Gordon we'll check on progress at the end of the day, on our way home. As we walk to the end of town, at the end of the main street, which is where the mine is, Dad gets very chatty. I think he's looking forward to work. Well, that is the whole point of the trip – and the beach vacation of course.

I am carrying a box of Dad's work stuff. Dad is carrying a pretty heavy case so we're making slow progress down the street.

Dad apologizes. "You won't mind another few days here, Thanh? It's not the most exciting place, but …"

"Nothing you can do about it," I say plainly.

I don't tell him that I don't know what's going to happen next and how I really like that about the whole trip. I can't say it's exciting but it's kind of fun and not how I usually spend my vacations.

Still, when Dad repeats "It doesn't matter," about getting to that fantastic beach, I catch his eye and tell him that it does matter. I know that's what he wants to hear – finally. Dad has this stupid idea that nothing matters to me.

I am suddenly jolted out of my happy little thoughts by a wailing siren. Dad begins to frown, but that's nothing new. He quickens his pace.

"I wonder what that is?" he asks, but I am not expected to answer. I feel and look alarmed.

"It's probably just a bell for the night shift," Dad assures me.

I know this is not true. It's not a bell for a start and it's too scary a sound for a bell that means you can stop work, plus Dad has quickened his pace an awful lot. I am almost running to keep up with him. There is a crowd gathering at the mine ahead. Dad glances at me. We both know there is something wrong. Dad doesn't need to tell me.

Everyone looks worried and there are distant voices yelling. But mostly people are looking expectantly, waiting for something to happen, or someone to explain what is happening. We stop at the gates. The siren has stopped. There are too many people and Dad needs to get inside. I wait there with the crowd.

"You stay here, Thanh. Don't move. I'll find someone," he barks at me. He takes his case with him.

I don't move. I stay where I am although I am constantly jostled by people. I don't move although I know no one – until Gordon arrives and whacks me on the back as if I were his best buddy.

"Where's your old man?" he asks. He pats the box. "Doesn't he need this?"

"For what? He's got his case and his backpack anyway," I shout.

Gordon shrugs.

I didn't think Dad was much good after accidents had already happened. I was sure that an accident had happened. In fact I was a bit worried that Dad was a safety inspector and this had happened. I felt that maybe he'd be held responsible. And if I hadn't wanted to come on the trip, Dad would have done his safety checks and this would never have happened, although I didn't know what had happened anyway. Well that's how my mind worked.

I couldn't see Dad anywhere and Gordon kept going on about how my dad would be involved in some kind of rescue. I couldn't see that. Dad took hours to set up his equipment. He told me when I begged him to let me come on this trip.

"I'll take all morning just checking it's ready to go. You'll be so bored. I can't think why you'd want to come except that you don't know what it's like. It's really dull and boring and the weather's sure to be bad. You'd be better off going to the school vacation program. Your mom told me they've got day trips to see films and go rock-climbing, and then she can pick you up after work and it's just like it always is."

This is what Dad told me and by this time he had such a tone in his voice that I didn't really think I wanted to go. You know how it is. I did end up going, of course, and I think Mom had something to do with it.

Chapter Six

Things That Matter II

I open my backpack and take out what I need. There is no time to get back to Thanh and tell him what's happening. One of the lifts is stuck. Simple, not an uncommon problem, really. Bad timing on my part. It isn't my field of expertise once matters get this far, but I can always tell them (the rescuers, the emergency squad – where were they?) how and why something has happened. I can hardly undo the zip on my backpack. I am so nervous. Everyone seems to think that I need to be lowered on top of the lift for a closer look. Yes, I am going to have company on this awful journey, but it isn't enough for me. I hate going underground. In fact, I have an awful fear of dark, confined spaces. I can check well enough from here, I could tell them. I like to think that when you're a safety expert, people believe what you say. Until something goes wrong.

I can feel my face flushing red with the prospect of being in a small, dark place. It doesn't help that everyone is watching me, as if I know something. But all I know is this terrible fear. Or was I just hot because someone had fastened a heavy helmet to my head? Did I say I hated going underground? No, that's not true. I am terrified, and I begin to fear that my breathing is coming in short but loud gasps. I listen to my breathing and it's true. It is very shallow. I think someone might notice how I sound. The more I think about it, the worse it sounds. I am sweating so much that I have to take off my helmet – and that's a struggle – to wipe my dripping brow. My hair is wet and I fumble foolishly with the helmet. I think they might know I don't want to go down there. They must realize that I'm fumbling and fooling around because I am scared. I can't look anyone in the eye. I fiddle with the orange overalls I've been made to wear. I don't want to go down there but I guess you realize that much, even if they don't.

I look around for Thanh and that's when someone finally asks me if something is wrong.

"I'm looking for my son. He's near the gates," I mumble. I can feel a headache coming on. I'd give anything to be a truck driver, on the road, window down, free … as free as one can be. I can see Thanh come bounding over but he has to keep a safe distance. He watches me expectantly, too. I wave at him and try my last resort once again. And I don't know why, but I am lucky.

"Try one more time, just push the buttons. They do get stuck in damp weather," I urge them to try pushing the lift buttons one more time.

Yes, I am lucky. There is a stirring, a thud, then a clunking as the lift stirs into action and eventually reaches the top. I can hardly smile but the joy on other faces more than makes up for my efforts.

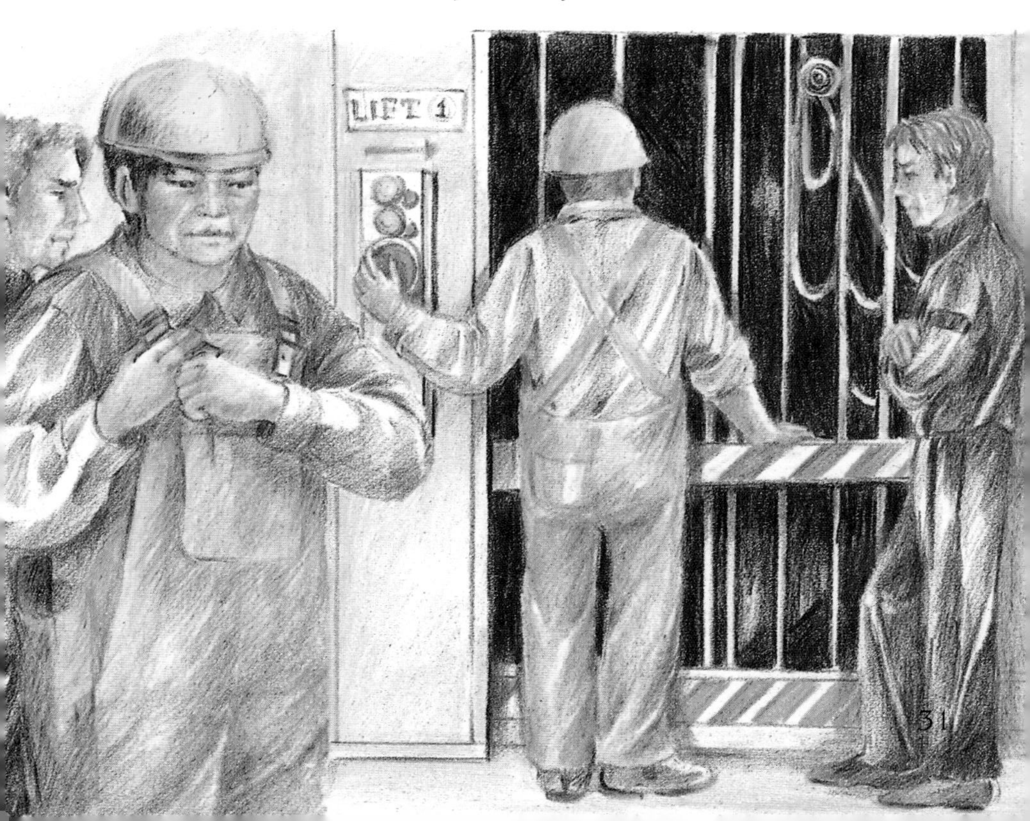

People surge toward the lift and I retreat. Crowds are too much for me and I do seem to be in line for congratulations that I don't deserve.

"Dad! Dad!"

It is Thanh calling. He rushes up to me, grabbing my arms, shaking me. Thanh is beaming. I have never seen him so happy. I put my arms around his shoulders. He must think I have helped. He must be proud of me. Well, it was a good suggestion about trying the buttons one more time. I would have gone down there though. But it never hurts to try one more time.